THUNDER AT GETTYSBURG

by Patricia Lee Gauch

Illustrated by Stephen Gammell

A BANTAM SKYLARK BOOK®

NEW YORK • TORONTO • LONDON • SYDNEY • AUCKLAND

The names Seminary Ridge, Cemetery Hill, Cemetery Ridge, and even Little Round Top did not exist as proper names before the battle, but for clarity, they have been so used in this book. Too, while the incidents involving Bobby Schultz, the Jenning girls, and Danny are true, the names are fictional. All other names are real.

The drawings by Stephen Gammell were done in 1974.

RL 2, 005–008

THUNDER AT GETTYSBURG

*A Bantam Skylark Book/published by arrangement with
G. P. Putnam's Sons*

PRINTING HISTORY
*Coward, McCann & Geoghegan edition published 1975
G. P. Putnam edition published 1990
Bantam edition/November 1991*

ISBN 0-553-15951-8

Published simultaneously in the United States and Canada.

*Bantam Books are published by Bantam Books, a division of Bantam
Doubleday Dell Publishing Group, Inc. Its trademark, consisting of the
words "Bantam Books" and the portrayal of a rooster, is Registered in U.S.
Patent and Trademark Office and in other countries. Marca Registrada.
Bantam Books, 666 Fifth Avenue, New York, New York 10103.*

PRINTED IN THE UNITED STATES OF AMERICA

CWO 0 9 8 7 6 5 4 3 2 1

FOR JEAN FRITZ

ACKNOWLEDGMENTS
I wish to thank Thomas J. Harrison,
Chief of Environmental Planning and Research
at the Gettysburg National Park, Frederick
Tillberg, Park Historian (now retired), and
J. William Long, Adams County Historical
Society, for their technical assistance.

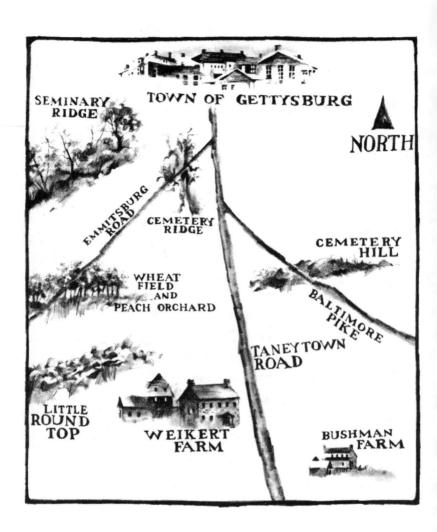

CONTENTS

1. THE FIRST DAY
July 1, 1863

BAROOM

"Pa! Ma!

Come quick. It's starting,"

Tillie yelled

as she pulled up her skirts

and took the stairs two by two.

She wasn't going to miss this.

Bobby Schultz had already

climbed into his loft to watch.

The Jenning girls were on their porch roof.

Flocks of folk were watching

and waving

right from High Street.

But Tillie knew where she was heading.

Her own attic.

Quickly she grabbed a chair
and pulled it up to the skylight.
She looked away over the alleys
and roofs and gardens
of Gettysburg.
She could see so clearly,
and sure enough, there they were.
Swarms of blue soldiers—her soldiers—
and swarms of gray
melting toward Seminary Ridge,
just west of town.
And horsemen in rows.
And there, spinning out behind them,
wagon after wagon after wagon.
"Close your mouth, Till,"
her father said from the doorway.
"You'll catch a fly!"

But Tillie couldn't help it.
A week ago she had wished
for Union troops to fight the Rebels.
Wished hard.
Now here they were, finally fighting them.
Her ma and pa talked a lot
about this war.
They said black men and women
and children wouldn't be slaves
ever again
if the Union won.
They said America wouldn't be split
in two if the Union won.
But Tillie didn't know
so much about that.
All she knew for sure was
Snap Rouzer and Davey Robinson
and a whole lot of other Gettysburg boys

went off to fight this war.
Then, a week ago—
with all those boys gone—
raggedy, gray-coated Rebel soldiers
came shouting through town.
They stole flour and meat
and shoes and hats and whiskey.
And they stole Tillie's horse, Danny.
The townsmen took up their pickaxes
and pitchforks,
their shovels and rusty guns.
But that didn't do any good.
The Rebs—that's what they called them—
stole the town dry.
And they rode Danny
so hard he died.
Pa touched Tillie's hand.
He was good at reading her thoughts.

Maybe he could read
that she wasn't going to move
from the window until the blues
beat the grays!
BAROOM! BAROOM!
Tillie's chair trembled under her.
Puffs of smoke coated
the hill like mist.
Tillie hung her head out the window.
The long rows of blues and grays
were bending.
CAK! CAK!
They were shooting!
"Good!" Tillie whispered.
Her father seemed awfully quiet.
Tillie couldn't read his thoughts
so well,
but she was excited.

What a great place to watch a war!
Now the lines seemed to be breaking.
Grays rushing down the hill,
blues climbing up,
horses running wild,
and cannons like thunder rumbling
over and over.
It seemed like such thundering
had to come to something—
any moment—right before her eyes.
Tillie stretched higher,
when suddenly a voice called out.
"James Pierce!"
Tillie's pa turned.
It was their neighbor Henny Schriver
and her two little girls.
Henny was as white as washed linen.
"This battling has put
the fear of the devil in us, James,

and I don't see no end to it.
I got to get away—
out of town—
to Mother's farm, where it's safe."
Tillie wasn't sure why Henny was
telling Pa.
"And I need help with the small ones,"
Henny went on.
"Perhaps . . . could Tillie come?"
Now Tillie understood!
"The battle's not in town, Henny,"
Pa was saying,
"but . . . well, yes, yes, of course
Tillie can go. "
"But, Papa," Tillie burst out,
"this is such a good spot,
and just now, when it looks as if something
is happening . . . "
"Tillie!" Ma warned.

"Pack a dress."

"No, ma'am," Tillie said, trying to sound respectful,

"I'll be back this day."

She wasn't going to miss all this for long.

2. ESCAPE TO WHAT?
Afternoon of the First Day

It was July hot.
Tillie could feel her face redden
as she tugged little Sarah
over Cemetery Hill behind Henny
and Molly.
The cannon was still rumbling.
Shots were still cracking.
But she didn't know
what was going on.
She was going to a farm!
With the chickens and cows!
Tillie picked up her skirts
and tried to catch up,
but it wasn't easy.
Yesterday's rain had turned

Taneytown Road
into a mud path.
She could feel the mud squeeze
around her shoe buttons.
Suddenly a Union soldier rode by.
Tillie jumped to one side.
She got splattered just the same.
What are you doing on this side
of town anyway? Tillie thought
as she wiped off her cheek.
Now ahead a column of Union bluecoats
were marching—almost running—
toward her,
four by four by four.
Tillie pulled Sarah into the field,
stepping backward to see
whether Snap Rouzer or Davey Robinson
were there.

They'd put up a good fight, sure.
But the lines seemed to fly by,
and Tillie nearly backed into a wagon
clattering down the road.
It was a white wagon,
carrying a soldier,
a bleeding soldier?
Tillie tried to see,
but the wagon rumbled by too fast.
Too fast.
Suddenly everyone seemed in such a hurry.
But why?
Wasn't the rumbling still on the west side
of town?
Weren't the shots still far away?
Tillie even felt herself
begin to run,
though she didn't know why.

And when they stopped
for a drink, a soldier yelled at them.
"You can't stop here, not now. Where are
you about?"
"Weikerts'," Henny told him.
Almost angrily he hailed a wagon.
"Take them to Weikerts'.
Hurry. "
Now Tillie's heart pounded.
The horse splattered through the mud.
She squeezed down,
but she could feel the mud
rain on her
and her blue cotton dress.
She felt as if she were being
swept up.
After some wild minutes
the driver splashed to a sudden
stop.

Finally, the Weikerts' farm.
Or was it?
Tillie could hardly see
the gray stone house,
and she couldn't see one cow or
one chicken.
Only soldiers in blue,
on the porch,
by the barn.
Soldiers on Taneytown Road, marching two
and two and two toward her.
All hurrying.
And Mrs. Weikert running
toward the wagon.
"Henny? Tillie?"
Mrs. Weikert climbed right into the wagon
to hug Henny's little girls.
"How did you get past them!"

Henny looked puzzled.

"Past who?" she asked.

"Past the Rebels. Or . . . don't you know?
The Rebels are sweeping through
Gettysburg, right now.
You must have missed them by a breath!"

Tillie sat down hard on the side board.
The rebels in town? With her mother and
father . . .

But Mrs. Weikert pushed a bucket at her.

"There's no time for sitting, girl.
We've got wounded coming in
to the house
to the barn,
and these men marching need water."

Tillie stood up slowly.

"And be quick," Mrs. Weikert said.
"The Rebels are firing on

Cemetery Hill now,
and if these Yanks don't get there
to help stop them,
those Rebs will come marching
right down Taneytown Road."
Tillie took the bucket and ran.
Maybe, just maybe, she wouldn't
get home tonight after all.

3. TRAPPED
July 2, 1863

Tillie spit on her hands,
but it didn't help much.
They were raw as wet hide.
And no wonder.
She had carried 46 buckets of water
to 632 soldiers—or thereabouts—
in five hours!
But there was no stopping
to worry about it.
There was no stopping to worry
about anything.
Not about her mother and father
trapped in Gettysburg with the Rebels.
Not about the soldiers being brought

into the barn and house
broken and bleeding.
Not even whether the Rebels
would come marching right down
Taneytown Road.
There simply was no time.
Even that night, nearly all the
shooting stopped
but nothing else did.
"Hurry, Tillie, rip cloths for the nurses."
"Over here, Tillie, this bread needs
punching."
"Quick, Tillie, fill these kettles
for the doctor. "
And again in the morning
the battle didn't start up right away,
but everything else did.
Tillie was running to the barn,
back to the kitchen,

over to the spring,

stirring,

ripping,

pulling,

pushing.

Until a few minutes before four o'clock.

Then Tillie hurried

to lead two officers to the roof.

They wanted to see as far as they could.

"There!" the colonel said, pointing.

There what? Tillie wondered.

She tried to see.

Far, far down Taneytown Road

she could see swarms of blue on

Cemetery Hill.

Yes, and there—closer—

along Cemetery Ridge,

lines of Union blue.

But the colonel wasn't pointing that way.

He was pointing at the hill

right behind the Weikerts' farm,
Little Round Top he was calling it.
Tillie smiled.
She and her friend Becky had had a picnic
in those rocks once.
But the colonel wasn't smiling.
"We keep that hill or lose the day!"
he said.
The Union couldn't lose again!
And Tillie almost told him.
She almost told him it wasn't
even that hill the Rebs wanted.
They wanted Cemetery Hill.
But that was when it happened.
Four o'clock.
BAROOOOMMMM
BAROOOOOOOMMMM

Cannon thunder rolled over the house—
over the house—
and suddenly Tillie knew the colonel was
right.
The Rebels must want both hills,
and they wanted Little Round Top now.
She knew something else.
She and Henny and the girls hadn't escaped
the battle at all. It was here.
Now.
And from that minute everything started
to go crazy.
Downstairs everyone was still running,
only faster.
"Here, Tillie, hot beef tea for the barn,"
Henny shouted, running into the kitchen.
Tillie burst full wind for the big red barn.

Soldiers started running right past her
toward the hill,
but Tillie couldn't stop to look.
On the way back she had to look.
A lieutenant was yelling at a young soldier
crawling on the ground.
"Get up, coward!"
The lieutenant kicked him.
Once. Twice.
"Get up and fight!"
Tillie's head spun.
That was a Union lieutenant kicking
his own soldier!
"Tillie!" Henny shouted.
Tillie bit her lip and started to run
back when—
BAROOOM
A shell burst right over the farmhouse,

shattering its metal over the field.
Tillie buried herself in the grass,
but she looked up when she heard
a Union soldier shouting at his horse.
"Giddyap!" he shouted.
The horse backed up.
SWIP!
The officer whipped the horse.
It reared and twisted.
SWIP! SWIP!
That's what the Rebs had done to
her horse, Danny.
The same thing!
Tillie suddenly stood up
and ran at him.
"Stop it!" she yelled.
But another shell screamed overhead,
bursting in midair,

and Henny came running to her.
She pulled Tillie toward the house.
"We're getting out . . .
to the Bushman farm.
We've heard the Rebs have taken
the peach orchard
and the wheat field,
and they're starting up
the other side of Little Round Top now.
The shells are already too close!"
Tillie and Henny joined the girls
and some wounded soldiers huddled
on the porch.
"Ready?" Mrs. Weikert whispered. "Run!"
Tillie squeezed Sarah's hand and ran.
A shell whistled over them,
but they ran and ran and ran.
"Down!" Mrs. Weikert shouted.

Another shell burst.
"Go!"
Tillie started again,
tumbling through the weeds,
down a hill and over a field.
Her side hurt from running.
Finally she could see the Bushman
farm ahead.
"Run, Sarah," she whispered.
But suddenly Farmer Bushman came
running toward them.
He was waving his hands crazily.
"Go back!" he shouted.
"The cannonballs are starting
to pass right over your place!
They're starting to land right here!"
Go back?
Tillie couldn't believe it.

She sank down into the weeds
with Sarah beside her,
but Mrs. Weikert shouted at them.
"Get up, Tillie! Sarah!"
She was as strong as any sergeant.
"Run!"
Tillie pulled Sarah up and started
to run again.
She could taste the smoke
and it stung her eyes,
but at last she could see Weikerts' again.
The door was already open.
They were nearly safe.
Mrs. Weikert ran into the house.
Henny made it.
But, all at once, Tillie stopped.
Soldiers were running down from the gap
next to Little Round Top—

Rebel soldiers.
And now from around the barn
a fife and drum and . . .
Union soldiers.
She pulled Sarah behind the well.
They couldn't make the house.
A Reb leaped the stone fence
just across the field.
CAK! A shot cut him down.
Two more Rebs leaped over.
CAK! CAK!
They crumpled like puppets.
Tillie crouched in the grass.
She could feel Sarah shaking beside her.
Bullets hissed across the field.
One, two, three, four,
five more Rebels fell.
Like puppets.

Finally the blues started marching
in a wavy line.
The blues and grays were fighting
hand to hand.
But Tillie kept looking at one of the Rebs
lying in the field.
He was bleeding from his nose
and mouth.
He would never get up again.
Never.
"Make a run for it, Tillie!"
Henny yelled from the doorway.
Tillie didn't know if she could move.
The bullets were still humming.
Everything was so crazy, so mixed up.
But she got to her knees.
"Ready, Sarah," she whispered. "Go!"
They dashed for the door

and kept running
through the dining room,
through the kitchen,
down, down into the cellar.
Right off Henny
settled Sarah and Molly on a mat,
then she started crawling around
helping the wounded.
But not Tillie.
Not this time.
She felt warm tears on her face.
They dropped off her nose,
but she didn't even bother
with them.
I'm not going to move again,
she promised herself.
Not for tea. Or water.
Or cannonballs.

Not one inch.
She didn't even move
when after some time
she noticed a soldier in the corner
near her.
"They say we've stopped 'em,"
he whispered.
"Pardon?" Tillie said.
"They're still fighting
on Cemetery Hill . . . but
we've stopped the Rebs at
Little Round Top."
"I guess I forgot
about winning Little Round Top,"
Tillie admitted.
She started to turn away,
when she saw his arm and side.
They were bleeding terrible.
"You live here?" he asked.

"No."

"Just helping?"

"Sort of." She guessed
that wasn't a lie.

"Well, you're a brave one,"
he said.

"No," she said. "I want it
to stop."

The soldier half grinned.

"Oh, I do, too, little one."

She looked at him sitting
in the shadows.

He looked so hurt.

"Would you like some . . . bread
. . . or water?"
she asked suddenly.

"Oh? Yes . . . yes,
bread would be good."

Tillie crawled over to the cellar kitchen
and back in three seconds flat.
His lips seemed to taste
each crumb.
Then he closed his eyes.
His head sagged and his hand
fell on Tillie's arm.
She let it stay.
Only once he looked up.
"Come see me in the morning,
will you, little lady?"
"Oh, I will," Tillie whispered.
"I will."

4. NO RUMBLING/NO SHOOTING
July 3, 1863

First thing in the morning
Tillie took Mrs. Weikert's big blue cup
filled with steaming tea downstairs.
The soldier would like that,
she knew.
Tillie was happy to see him
still sleeping near the doorway.
"Sir!" she said quietly.
But he didn't move.
It was as if he were frozen.
"Sir?" Tillie said again, louder.
Her stomach started to hurt.
"General Weed's dead, miss,"
a soldier said. "He died some time
in the night."

The hurt wouldn't go away.
When the officers put the two cannons
on either side of the house
and told everyone to get to a safe place,
Tillie just followed everyone else
into the wagon.
She could hear the drums
rolling,
the fifes trilling,
and she could hear a low rumble
of voices like leaves in the wind
down Cemetery Ridge way.
But she rode silently,
down Taneytown Road, over the cross road,
toward Baltimore pike.
On the way she saw some prisoners.
They looked plain tired.
Not so bad or so awful

as plain tired.
A lot like General Weed had looked.
The wagon finally stopped
at a little gray farmhouse beyond the pike.
It was full,
packed like a chicken house.
It seemed as though all the farm folk
and wounded near the battleground
had fled there.
And more kept coming,
each telling what he had seen or heard.
"Well," said one, "all I saw was smoke,
billowing smoke,
but I heard there's some rebel general—
Picket they called him—
sweeping his men across
Cemetery Ridge like . . .
a giant wave.
I do believe nothing will stop those Rebs!"

"Maybe," another said.
"But did you see those Yanks
lining up behind that stone wall
on Cemetery Ridge,
like it was a fortress."
"I did!" a third man yelled out.
"And I saw a gunner there
in a copse of trees just firing
and firing. "
A latecomer put in quietly,
"They were fighting hand to hand
when I saw them.
Hand to hand.
Thousands of 'em.
Thousands and thousands of American men,
fighting each other."

Tillie burst out the back door.
The doctors were setting up straw mats
right outside for the wounded.
She caught up with Henny,
who was carrying water.
Tillie started carrying water, too.
Then she helped the farmer's wife
rip some linen for bandages.
Then she helped a nurse carry blankets.
After that she cut bread
and passed it to the men.
Finally Henny told her, "Sit
for a minute, Till!"
"No, ma'am," Tillie said.
She didn't want to,
and she wouldn't.

Even this far away the rumbling
went on and on as though it would finally
split the sky.
But near three o'clock
Tillie felt the air get still.
Sunday morning still.
There was no rumbling or shooting
or shouting.
Nothing.
Some folks started waiting
by the fence or over by the hill,
but the Weikerts and Tillie started
back to the farm.
A misty dusk was settling
when they walked into the yard,
but Tillie could see.
Wounded men,
their arms and legs broken

or bleeding or gone,
lay scattered all over the yard.
Like bits of cloth.
Near the barn. Under the trees.
Everywhere.
Many calling for help.
And behind them near the fence,
a growing pile of long pine boxes.
Coffins.
Nobody could speak. Not Mrs. Weikert
or Henny, not the girls. Not Tillie.
And then a soldier passed them at the well.
"We won!" he said. "General Lee and
his Rebels
aren't in retreat yet,
but everyone's saying it's over.
We've won!"
Tillie sat down on the wet grass.

For a long time she sat and thought.
About General Weed's hand
on her arm,
about the men lying outside on the
straw mats.
About the smoke, the screaming bullets,
bursting shells,
about . . . this yard . . . now.
It was better to win.
But look what had happened.
Dear God, look what happened.

5. SOMETHING TO CELEBRATE
July 4, 1863

The next day
in a drizzling rain
General Lee
and his wagons of broken men
wound out through the hills
like a sad gray ribbon
blown to the wind.
When they were gone,
Tillie climbed Little Round Top
and looked toward town.
She hadn't heard anything
about her ma and pa in three days.
Everyone said yesterday's battle
never reached into town,
but Tillie needed to see for herself.

What she saw didn't help.
The battle seemed to have swept
everywhere
like a terrible storm.
There and there and there
soldiers still lying in
burned black fields,
the way they died.
Yanks and Rebs.
Horses, stiff and still.
Broken wheels.
Overturned wagons.
Funny how a tipped wagon
could make her feel so peculiar—
so empty.
Seeing it all only made her worry more.

At the farm—
in between the running and carrying—
she started asking
anyone coming from town,
"You see a red house in town?
You see a man and woman name of Pierce?"
"Sure, in my spare time I had a tea party
with them," one soldier told her.
Another laughed at her.
"I seen twenty houses, each with a man
and woman doing right well. Pick one."
It seemed as if no one
had really seen her ma and pa.
Then it started to rain harder.
Tillie and Henny were running
to the barn with candles
when a wagon stopped.
"You Tillie? Tillie Pierce?" a soldier yelled.

She didn't answer.
She was tired of tricks.
"Your mother and father
said to tell you they're all right,
and to hurry home."
Tillie felt those stupid tears
dropping off her nose.
"How do I know it's my mother
and father?"
"You got the only red house
in town with two linden trees
right out front?"
Tillie couldn't help smiling.
"I do," she said. "I do."
"Then it's your folks, all right."
Tillie started to laugh
and spank the mud off
her dirty blue cotton dress.

"I'm only three days late,"
she said.
Henny laughed, too, and put her arm
around Tillie.
"I don't think they'll mind a bit."
They started walking to the house.
"I'll never forget this Fourth of July,
Henny. And not the first of July
or the second or the third either."
"None of us will, Till."
Tillie stopped.
"I don't think I want to forget,
do you, Henny?"

A NOTE FROM THE AUTHOR

The battle of Gettysburg was an accident. Neither the Rebel Confederate troops nor the Union troops wanted to fight at Gettysburg, but when a Rebel infantry ran into a Union cavalry on July 1, 1863, the battle began.

Hundreds of townspeople were caught in the surprise. Early the first day many found a comfortable spot, an upstairs window or loft, and watched the battle as they would a circus. But by midafternoon every man and woman and child knew this was a real and terrible battle, and by the second day many had, like fourteen-year-old Tillie Pierce, found themselves helplessly drawn into the very battle itself.

Early in the fighting the Weikert farm was used as a hospital, but after the first day the battle swung from the north to the south, and the farm soon became part of the battlefield itself.

The farm still stands today, couched on the east slope of Little Round Top, a hill important to the Union defense in 1863 because along with Cemetery Hill and Culp's Hill it commanded high ground. Cannon fire was lobbed over the house. Attacks occurred within feet of it. Bullets hummed around it even as the cooking and the nursing and the operating went on. Few civilians had a closer look at the real face of war than Tillie and the little band of people at the Weikert house.

Tillie Pierce Alleman never did forget those July days. This story is based on a book she herself wrote in 1889. It was called *At Gettysburg. Or What I Saw and Heard at the Battle of Gettysburg.* Other townspeople wrote, too, and reporters and historians. They seemed to be saying over and over: remember, the battle did help cripple the Rebel Confederate army, but the cost to both sides—and to the country—was immense. It was true. More than 150,000 American men had gone into battle, and in three days 50,000 had been killed, wounded, or were missing.

Gettysburg was called the turning point of the Civil War, but even the President, Abraham Lincoln, wanted to make certain no one forgot this battle or why it was fought. He came to Gettysburg several months later and said to the people:

> *It is . . . for us to be here dedicated to the great task remaining before us, that we here highly resolve that these dead shall not have died in vain, that this nation shall have a new birth of freedom, and that this government of the people, by the people, for the people, shall not perish from the earth.*
>
> *—from* The Gettysburg Address